WONDER AND THE SAINT

CHRISTINE CRONIN

Wonder and The Saint © 2021 Christine Cronin

ISBN (Print): 978-1-09835-615-6
ISBN (eBook): 978-1-09835-616-3

To all the wonders and saints in the world
who came before or are yet to be realized

Dear John,
    Thank you for being
a person who has always
shared their love of
literature and meaningful
conversation with me.
May we continue to follow
our dreams and have
the courage to honor our hearts

Love
Tine

THE ENDING

Most people think that when something ends, it's over. I think an ending means something new is starting. This story starts with an ending, because endings are beginnings, and beginnings are endings. It was an ending to Wonder's last ten years of practicing patient treatment in physical therapy, and an ending to the way the Saint operated in his career for most of his adult life.

This is a **true story**. These characters really exist, but I left them unnamed for a variety of reasons. The first reason is to respect their privacy and the fact that they are not people who relish a spotlight. Second, sometimes we see others as the exception to the rule. We say, "I can never do that," or "How do they do that?" If we can see something in another person it means it is possible and already exists within us. Lastly, I believe there are saints and wonders all around us. All we have to do is become aware and open up to see the beauty that abounds. Not to mention, every hero has an alias. Maybe Clark Kent or Diana Prince live in your neighborhood?

The Saint comes from the field of Education, Recreation, and Health and Fitness. Wonder comes from the medical field and the practice of Physical Therapy (specialist in human movement and restoring quality of life). They come together in a school setting to pilot a new well-being program for children. This is their story. They hope you enjoy it!

The Saint ·

The first thing I noticed about the Saint was that his eyes sparkle with joy and his smile lights people up. The second thing I noticed was his kindness. The way he practiced kindness obliterated my belief that kindness had finite parameters, challenged my own capacity for kindness, and made me desire more kindness in the world. The third thing I noticed was the way he changed his environment. His presence created an energy that enabled people to become.

Notice the word "become." The Saint did not demand you follow his way. He created a space for you to "become" who you are meant to be. In the last three weeks of my first year with the Saint, I remember feeling more myself than I had ever felt in my entire adult life. If that isn't miraculous, I don't know what is.

The Saint isn't actually a person who would call himself a saint. His humility would limit that from occurring, and there is a slight chance he doesn't even know he is one. If you get closer, sit quietly, lean in, ask questions, and wait patiently... you'll be amazed to find you're with a saint.

You might be wondering how I know I was with an actual saint. I was wondering that too. They say in order to become a saint, you have to perform three miracles. I watched more than three unfold in my time with the Saint. It's also been said that a saint is just a person who is excellent at being a human being. There were miracles and there was excellence, but this story isn't about that. It is about what happens when Wonder and the Saint walk together for a while with kind hearts and open minds and how the world changes.

Wonder ··

I am Wonder. I started asking "why?" at three years old, and never stopped. I love questions, because I love learning, life, and people. After asking questions for almost four decades, I've noticed that not all people welcome those who *wonder*. My mind is in a state of wonder at almost all times. I am truly interested in everything happening around me. If I am not directly asking, I'm constantly observing and formulating questions and theories in my mind. It is an absolute delight when I find someone willing to entertain my curiosity.

As a person who loves learning, listening, and asking questions, I know what it feels like to be discouraged, shut down, and silenced. People can silence us in a multitude of ways—from their body language, dismissive, hurtful and sarcastic remarks, or choosing no response. I once heard that, "Resistance to questioning is one of the first signs of an unhealthy relationship." I believe it, because I know that my most healthy and fulfilling relationships are met with reciprocal thoughtful questions and listening that lead to deeper understanding, awareness and connection.

I also recognize there were times I didn't ask questions at the right time, nor use the correct tone or context. I've made mistakes with the way I question. For example, I've asked questions in front of a group or when emotions are high, and that can feel like attacking. The most important parts of questioning for me are learning, understanding, and connecting. I have evolved as a question asker. I have become more patient, thoughtful and take great care in the way I ask questions. I try to wait for opportunities to arise instead of on my own agenda. I give more choice in my questions, such as, "When would be a good time to talk about this?" I can rapidly assess who will tolerate my questions and who will not.

Wondering lead me to the Saint. It was in being welcomed that I stayed. It was in a shared desire to question and find good, truth, and all that is loving and joyful in this life that we grew together. I would think it is safe to say, neither of us, nor the people we touched, will ever be the same.

We wanted to share our top ten lessons with everyone, in the hopes that it may provide a positive example of what can happen when people come together on the journey of life. With teachable spirits, open hearts and minds anything is possible!

LESSON 1

. . . .

"Prayer Is The Most Important Part of the Day."

The Saint always said, "Prayer is the most important part of the day." Now, I know what you might be thinking, "I don't pray," or, "I don't believe in God," or maybe, "I already do that." Whatever crosses your mind is just fine with me. I'm not trying to tell anyone what to do, because I wouldn't appreciate that either. I'm simply retelling the story I learned. Let me break down what "prayer" looks like to the Saint and how it might be applied to all people no matter their belief or disbelief.

Number one, it makes sense that the person who is the Saint says prayer is the most important part of his day. It just goes together. What is prayer? Prayer in this context is a conversation with God—not that this description clarifies anything. Let's try another way to look at it. Once a person asked what "My image of God is," because they said that would determine "everything!" Whoa! Determine everything? Heavy. I thought about my image of God. At first, I thought of a super old Dude who was sitting very far away with a kind of old, grumpy, judging face. I felt that I was not good enough and that I would never live up to Old Grandpa God. This was indeed my childhood imaginings of "God." Then I learned more about Jesus. I could really get on board because he loves people, questions, healing, women, outcasts, and liked to teach by the sea or escape up to the mountains to think and pray. His message was of unconditional love and forgiveness. I thought about how I had become successful in life and felt it had to do with the unconditional love and forgiveness my family and friends had shown me. Jesus made sense.

Because I wonder, I've read about people who had great wonder in them. A few of my favorites are; Martin Luther King Jr., Corretta Scott King, Mother Theresa, St. Ignatious, Gandhi, Tolstoy, Socrates, Marcus Aurelius, Confusicous, Thich Nhat Hanh, Mihaly Csikszentmihalyi and Black Elk of the Oglala Sioux. It seems great wonderers and inspirational leaders share similarities that are transcendent. Gandhi thought that if you want to know God, you have to be willing to look your enemy in the eye and love them as yourself. He also believed that God was "truth." Biblical references to what Jesus said were the two most important commandments were loving God with your whole being and loving your neighbor as yourself, including your enemies! MLK spoke of the interconnectedness of humanity and that hate cannot drive out hate, only love can. A priest once told me that, "God is love." Everything else is just humanity and religious interpretations. It seems like we have great thinkers and inspirational leaders throughout time leaning on similar themes of truth, love and peaceful-justice for all.

Now my image of God is one of the Creator, all that is good and beautiful springing forth from this universal desire for love, truth and peace. This is the source of unconditional love, forgiveness, compassion, and healing. This Creator or creative spirit is constantly seeking to connect with us, but often we are not open to the connection. The concept of God can get quite sticky. Many a human atrocity have been practiced in the name of God(s). Here is one additional clarifier that may help. I once heard someone say, "Everyone has a God. It is whatever they worship most." This statement gave me great pause. What do I worship most? Again, I could get on board with this and see it clearly. I have met very religious people who seemed quick to cast judgment, division, and exclusion. They didn't seem to be aligned with the belief system they practiced. Meanwhile, I have met kind hearted people, open to growth, and welcoming to all with healing hearts who claimed no God at all. Whether you come from an organized religion or none at all, let us pause to ask, "What do I worship most, in both action and word?" Is it fame, status, money, self-image, and accomplishments? Or, is it love, truth, acceptance, humility and authenticity? When we pause to ask what we worship most we will begin to find our answers and of course more questions.

Back to the Saint. He worshiped a God of relationship, with loving compassion for all. He worshiped an active and present life-giving God who was quick to forgive. He is both a healer and a teacher. In attempting to connect each day with this ideal, the Saint was indeed a person of relationship, compassion, love, service, forgiveness, and a healer and teacher. He ideally (remember—not perfect), set aside time each day to enter into a conversation with God. Not only was he speaking to God from his heart, but he was making time to look and listen for God in his day. He would sit outside at the end of his day, and practice something called the Examen. The Examen is a prayer technique developed by St. Ignatius of Loyola a long, long time ago. It is an enlightening way to build awareness and joy through a guided reflection on our day.

- It starts by quieting the mind and recognizing we are loved. When we feel loved, we act from places of care and compassion. When we feel hurt, we unfortunately are more likely to hurt others or ourselves. Pausing for a moment to feel love is inherently wise.

- Next, we review our day with gratitude and pay attention to our emotions. This is just plain smart. Gratitude is key to mental health, and improving our emotional intelligence is beneficial for everyone! We are pretty good at numbing and ignoring our emotions instead of paying attention to them. Tuning into our emotions is a way to listen to our internal guide.

- When we find an example of joy in our day, we pause and reflect longer on that period. Can we imagine it in our mind again, hold it longer, and then feel the emotion again—recalling as much detail as possible? We also recall where we felt tension, fear or anger. This may direct us to places of forgiveness as well as places in need of care and action.

- As we reflect on our day, we ask if we have been kind to others and open to growth? We also ask for forgiveness and the strength to forgive when we have errored, or we perceive a slight from another.

- We close by asking for encouragement and continued guidance in becoming the person we were made to be.

Both the Saint and I shared a commonality of practicing some form of active reflection, contemplation, and gratitude about life and our role in it. It was in the practice of daily contemplation that helped us grow and take action together in our journey.

1. Do I make time for quiet reflection, meditation, or prayer?

2. For what aspects of life am I grateful?

3. Where do I find joy in my day (life)?

LESSON 2

· · · · · · · · · · · · · · ·

"Live the Mission"

We had a mission statement at my work, but it was long and difficult to remember. There was no way I could recite it. When I met the Saint, it struck me that every person of all ages at his place of work could recite their mission. It was not long before I too had the school's mission statement memorized. Time was allotted at the beginning of the day to speak the mission statement aloud together. The day started in prayer, centered on a mission.

The mission statement wasn't something the Saint just memorized. It was something he lived and breathed. He put his whole heart, mind, body, and spirit into it. There was a point where I was almost annoyed by the amount of times the mission was referred to. "I get it!" I thought to myself, "Do we have to keep referring to it and talking about it?" Yes, we did. When things started to get difficult, complicated, or challenging, it was the mission that helped us find our way. If we didn't keep it at the forefront, if we didn't base every decision off of it, we could get lost. If the Saint wasn't perfectly aligned with the mission, he would not have been able to continue to perform to the ability he did with the passion, purpose, and grace he bestowed on others. In fact, this is why we connected so easily. At our hearts' centers, we were already living and working toward the mission. We were both striving to be aligned with the mission in a way that left little doubt about who we were and why we were here.

We both had different ways of carrying out, interpreting, and communicating the mission, but we knew exactly where we stood together. There was great trust, centeredness and togetherness from our belief in the mission and each other. Once I understood how important the mission was, and the Saints ability to be aligned with it to his very core I found the true power in the mission. I went home and thought about my family and myself. What will be our mission? How can we create one that helps us find our center, togetherness, and trust? What could we strive toward that will help us rise each morning, especially on the tough days? What will our beacon be in the storms?

I was finally able to come up with my personal mission and we are still fine tuning our family mission. My mission is to patiently, passionately, and purposefully, love, serve, and inspire those around me, but especially my family and friends. I repeat it to myself each morning. It is written on our fridge and bathroom mirror. I know that whatever curve balls life throws—from pandemics to role changes—I am capable of striving toward my mission in some small way, each day. It is my reason for rising.

1. What is my mission?

2. Does my place of work/family have a mission?

3. Does my way of being align with my mission?

LESSON 3

. . . .

"Greetings Matter"

The Saint's smile was contagious. If I close my eyes and imagine the Saint smiling, I find myself smiling. WOW! That's power—the ability to make someone smile just at the imaginings of their smile. The Saint greeted every person like they were the most important person in the universe, and he meant it. I found myself feeling joyfully uplifted upon seeing the raised welcoming arms, giant smile, and sparkling eyes of the Saint. My day was better when I was greeted by him. I was kinder in my subsequent interactions. It wasn't just the smile, the intention, or the welcoming body language. The Saint called me by name. He called everyone by name. Sometimes, he messed up. He would laugh, correct himself, or be corrected and carry on.

"How long have you been working on names?" I asked.

"Since I was about your age and I noticed that people in the Senior Center responded really well to hearing their name."

"Yes," I think in my mind, "I still have time to practice names and get as good as the Saint at greeting people and sharing joy."

"You can't be afraid to mess up though." he replies. "Once I called a guy by the wrong name for two months before he told me differently, but then I never got it wrong again." he says with a smile. He is not afraid to laugh at himself. Laughter is encouraged.

I think of all the times I have not called a person by their name. I know that it was fear limiting me. I was afraid of failing, and my fear of getting it wrong meant I missed an opportunity for connection. One of the Saint's super powers is his ability to greet, call by name and welcome all. I know that I too, could have this ability, but I will have to overcome fear and push myself out of my comfort zone. Still, I know what it feels like to be greeted by a saint, and I know that if he can do it, so can we.

1. Am I aware of how I greet others?

2. How do I make people feel when I greet them?

3. Who is someone whose greeting elicits joy in me? Have I told them?

LESSON 4

. . . .

"Leave our Armor at the Door – Be Authentic"

Most of my adult life was spent in the medical field, which requires a high level of care, a certain amount of healthy detachment, and a lot of problem solving. In helping guide others through the healing process, it is important to listen well to their story as that is the beginning of finding the solution. Listening requires a large amount of setting the self aside. I was good at setting aside myself to listen. Sharing my own story is rarely appropriate or opportune while treating patients.

When I came to the Saint, I was taking everything I learned in the medical field to help promote healthy habits earlier in the education system. I knew what I knew well, but had no experience in taking my ideas into a school system with a much younger and larger audience. The Saint welcomed every new idea with grace, gratitude, and enthusiasm. He was so welcoming and encouraging, I found myself speaking up more and more. Soon, new ideas were rapidly forming in this healthy, inspiring environment.

I'm a person just like everyone else, which means I have challenging days, question my ability, and I make mistakes. However, I'm also a person who others look up to, and can begin to believe doesn't make mistakes, have bad days, and/or question my ability. For one of the first times in my life, instead of pretending everything was fine, I trusted the Saint enough to be very real and authentic. Each morning we greeted each other with joy and enthusiasm, but then honestly checked in on how the other was doing—and we honored that throughout our day.

As a mother of three young children, my mornings were always the toughest part of the day. They usually involved crying from at least one child (occasionally myself), resistance in leaving our home, running late (which made me feel anxious), and a car ride full of some sort of in-fighting. There were mornings I arrived at school feeling my patience was completely gone, and that was before starting work. In the past, I would have kept these intense feelings of struggle, failure, and questioning to myself. Instead, the Saint made me feel safe, seemed to understand, and desired for an authentic relationship with me.

I began to let the Saint know about the challenges of my morning when it was particularly rough. He listened well, affirmed me, and offered encouragement. I found that my ability to be myself and my turn-around from a rough morning was much quicker when I shared it with a friend. Soon, I felt lighter and had a greater ability to endure and be patient without having to carry the weight of my armor. My armor took the shape of putting up the image that I was okay, even if I wasn't. My armor can also take the shape of question asking. I can deflect anything that gets too close with a question that redirects the conversation. I can hide behind questions, or I can use them to grow in a relationship. When I wear my armor, it takes energy and requires a wall between myself and the outer world. There are times when it is appropriate, but not all the time—and especially not with the ones we love.

The Saint taught me to lay down my armor. He never asked me to lay down my armor. He never told me I could benefit from being more authentic. He was simply so kind, encouraging, and welcoming that he made me feel safe. He made me feel loved and accepted for exactly who I was, which enabled me to be exactly who I am. He was vulnerable with me, too. He shared his struggles, his challenges, and his triumphs. For the first time in a long time, I felt completely safe to be exactly who I was at work—not a version of myself, or someone else's expectation of me—simply me.

All of a sudden, my creative potential was bursting at the seams. I could reach places I had never imagined without the weight of armor. I was learning lessons I never could have seen or entered into before. We are both human, which means some days we put our armor back on. We created a wall to help us feel safer, and went back to our old strategies. Luckily, those moments were few and far between. After prayerful reflection, we often apologized the next day if we were defensive or not open to growth and receiving. When we apologized to each other, we were able to put down our armor once more and step into the sunlight, arms wide open with a smile greeting the day and all those in our path with gratitude.

1. What does my armor look like?

2. Is there anyone with whom I can lay down my armor?

3. Do others wear armor around me?

LESSON 5

. . . .

"Give Choice"

The Saint worked tirelessly to give people choices. He taught multiple grade levels which meant multiple stages of development, ability and personalities. Giving students choice meant more work for him, as he needed to be prepared for whatever the choice was.

I was not good at giving people choice. I liked my ideas, researched them well, and thought they were the best. Of course I did. I was coming from a field where I needed to know the right answer and prescribe the exact strategy to help "fix" something. I was not at all used to giving people options on how to fix themselves. I was used to being right, with an emphasis on that rightness being paramount to the success of patient outcomes. Yet, I saw that something is lost on us when we "tell someone" what to do. We either become the wielder of great power and create a victim mentality in the people we are "helping," or we take away their ownership and ability to feel control over their bodies and environment.

Here is an example of what I mean. In my work treating patients, if I noticed someone had a balance deficit, I would recommend balance exercises. I would choose a few of the top evidenced-based exercises, and tell the patient exactly what to do. Knowing what I know about the power of choice and its ability to improve well-being and accountability, I would do that differently now. I would let the patient know of the importance of balance and then I would have them choose two of their favorites out of three or four options.

The Saint revealed what current evidence (see the book *Drive* by Daniel Pink) and people with years of experience in education and motivation already know. People, of all ages, for all eternity, respond better when they feel they have some element of control in their lives and that they have the freedom to choose.

1. Do I give opportunities for choice in my interactions?

2. Do I feel like I have choice in my own day?

3. How do my choices affect myself and others?

LESSON 6

. . . .

"Teach What You Want to See"

I do not like yelling, nor being yelled at. In fact, it is a physiological painful response for me. I love listening. I have a fine-tuned ear, so yelling, or being yelled at actually hurts. I try not to raise my voice, but again, as a mother of three young children I have found there are times when I do, and times when the volume in our house is overwhelming.

The Saint was not a yeller. If he was, it would have been too painful for me to get close enough to learn. In fact, there were multiple opportunities when I might have raised my voice and he did the opposite. I was confused. Instead of trying to match or exceed the volume around him, he got quieter, calmer, and stood still with confidence and waited. After a few moments, he would capture his audience. Not only would he capture his audience, but he did it in a calm, kind, and considerate way. He did not diminish, single out, or demean a single person. Wow! I had never seen anything quite like it before, nor had I personally experienced it in my own educational or sport experience.

I knew people in leadership positions who singled out individuals in front of a group when mistakes were made. In their frustration, they made broad sweeping statements about the group, diminishing the ones who were putting forth great effort. For example "Nobody's listening," or "It doesn't feel like anybody wants to be here," or "Nobody's trying." When we make statements like this, we harm the people who are giving their best effort, and we do little to affect the ones who brought us to the point of speaking the words in the first place. I am guilty of this as well.

The Saint did not do this. I am sure at one point in his career he may have, but he often spoke of learning from his past mistakes and experiences. We were together at a time in his career where he had grown significantly from his past. He would teach people what he wanted to see, and that's what they would do. It was amazing! Of course, there were still people who were acting out or making other choices, but instead of focusing on what people were doing incorrectly, he emphasized what was happening that was positive.

For example, if somebody was engaging in disruptive side conversation while he was speaking, he would pause and then thank somebody who was listening well by giving a specific example. "I like how Sarah is looking right at me and showing me she cares by listening." Soon others would notice Sarah and try to emulate her good listening. He got to teach what skill/virtue he was hoping to see and speak words of kindness to initiate change.

I rarely shared what I was hoping to see with the people closest to me. How would they know what I was looking for, my hopes or expectations, if I couldn't even speak them aloud? What do I want to see? How could I start to express that in positive and clear ways with the people in my family, community, and work? Of course I would need to model exactly what I want to see.

The Saint made that quite clear—the way he hoped to be treated is how he treated everyone. He was respectful, forgiving, and graceful with a kind and loving heart. A tall order—that's why forgiveness and unconditional love (or positive regard) is imperative. We will all fall repeatedly short of this high bar, but if we can be loving and forgive ourselves and each other, we will rise higher each time we do. Most of the time, people rise up to the expectations we set for them. The Saint had a high bar, and he helped others get there through clear expectations, loving kindness, patience, and forgiveness.

1. What do I want to see in my life?

2. Am I a living example?

3. How can I express this?

LESSON 7

. . . .

"Humble Hearts- "We" Not "Me"

On the days the Saint would fall short of his expectations, he would say that his ego got in the way, or that he didn't make time to pray (or both). I don't think ego is inherently bad. I just think when we are more focused on what we want (vs need), and how our wants fit into the bigger picture, we can get in trouble. Often when we feel emotions like jealousy, anger, fear, and frustration we look at a scenario through our ego lens, versus our empathy lens. Instead of trying to see and feel from the perspective of the person(s) around us (empathy), we are seeing things only through our eyes and their direct immediate impact on us.

It is very natural to see life this way. It takes a lot of practice in gratitude, perspective taking, and thoughtful reflection to recognize when we are solely (I or Me) focused over "we" focused. We need to start with the "I" focus in life as we find our identity and grow as a person. If we cannot shift to a "we" focus, we will miss out on connection and meaningful relationships which are essential components of a full life.

The Saint had worked independently for a long time before I came on the scene to team up with him. He was used to having things being his, because there wasn't another co-worker with whom he shared a space. He welcomed me into his office and said, "This is ours." We replaced "mine" with "ours" and "I" with "we." Turns out, these subtle shifts in linguistics also shift our mind to focus more on the whole than our ego. There were times when he would naturally fall back and refer to something as "his" and I might cue him or he would catch himself and quickly correct to "us," "ours," or "we". It is amazing to think about how awesome the power of "we" is. "We" is not lonely, isolated or egotistical, it is powerful, strong, and community building.

I have noticed the people I look up to, connect with, and believe in, practice the art of humility. The funny thing is— most of us don't like to be humbled, myself included. Being humbled can be painful, uncomfortable, and challenging. The Saint worked hard to be humble, but he was similar to me in not enjoying being humbled. He was humbled a lot during our time together. He was used to being very physically strong, fit, and capable. He was used to functioning at a high capacity for long periods of time.

Age and injury will find all of us in our lifetime if we are fortunate enough to live that long. I met him when age, injury and cumulative life stressors came to a crescendo. He needed help in areas he never had before. He did not like to ask for help. This is a common theme in some of the finest helpers I have ever met—a strong desire to serve with much more resistance to being served. He asked me for help. I was honored.

The ability to serve someone I held in such high regard— to help a friend and person who had given so much for so many—was incredibly fulfilling. In the past, he would have looked at something heavy, wouldn't have thought twice about flinging it on his back and jogging off. Now he pauses, looks at me, and asks, "Can you get that please?" Humbling.

"Yes, absolutely." I would answer, and I would continue to lift, carry, pick up, run, listen, and try to predict all the ways I could help the Saint so that he could continue bringing joy to everyone. I realized that someday I would be humbled too. I also knew, when that time came, I would have the opportunity to become like the Saint. I will ask for help, recognize my areas of weaknesses, and teach and share what I have learned with the people around me. I realize being humbled will always represent a challenge, but I will look at it as the path to humility and grace, instead of something to wish away or avoid.

When we think of a saint, we might think of perfection. The Saint was far from perfect. He made a lot of mistakes in his life, and he would be the first to tell you that. What was cool about the mistakes was that he learned, grew, and changed as the result of the those experiences. It was not uncommon for him to say, "I'm sorry. I messed up." Not only did the Saint make mistakes, but for all the light he brought to others, he had his own struggles.

It's an interesting thing. Every saint I've read about had struggles with darkness. We will define darkness as those moments or periods in life of doubt, confusion, loneliness, fear, suffering, and uncertainty. Let's assume that each of us—and what it means to be human—struggle with light and dark. We could say we struggle with positive coping strategies and negative coping strategies, growth mindset and fixed mindset, hope versus despair, yin and yang. Let's assume every documented historical saint had a rough patch. Is it possible that to be an excellent human, we have to struggle at times, maybe even for very long periods of time? Perhaps then, just like the mistake was not to be avoided but to learn from, the struggle may be the path to fully recognizing the light.

What is means to be a saint is striving to be an excellent human. Striving to be an excellent human looks like authenticity, failure, forgiveness, compassion for all (including yourself), gratitude, and doing the best with what we have. The Saint made it okay to fail, to have fear, to question and doubt, to be humbled. Most importantly he taught me how to share those burdens so that the load was lighter and we could learn from the each other. He made it okay to make mistakes. This allowed greater daring, bigger sharing, and way more fun in life. Now a mistake was not a thing to fear, but a thing on which to reflect, grow, and learn from—and try again, with a new and improved approach.

There is a lot of pressure in our "U.S." culture toward perfection—from body image, to social media to who we see as role models. In my time with the Saint, I never once felt I needed to be perfect. He would encourage me before I was going to speak to an audience, or if I was nervous, by saying, "Just speak from your heart." Wow. I can't say I had heard that in my adult life either. "Just speak from your heart."

If I could put words to the way the Saint made me and others feel it would be; welcome, I love you just the way you are, speak from your heart, be kind and respectful, play together, I only want and desire what is best for you on your journey.

1. Do I speak from my heart?

2. What does humility look like?

3. Can I both give and receive help?

LESSON 8

. . . .

"Play"

"Would you like to play?" he asks.

"No thank you." I say, "I have too many things I need to do." He will ask me every day, and will give me many opportunities to say "Yes" or "No." My "no" response does not mean he will stop inviting me. He always invites everyone.

I do not always invite everyone. I do not stop to play often enough. The Saint kept asking me. One day, we are outside on a grass field. It is beautiful. He says, "Go long" and I start running and I keep running. He can throw a Frisbee (disc) really well. It's soaring through the sky. I am at a full sprint now, tracking it with my eyes over my shoulder as I run. Completely focused on the target, matching my speed to the expected flight path, I reach out for the disc and it bounces off my finger tips and lands in the grass. I am out of breath, bent over, and smiling. I grab the disc, run back, and hand it to him. "Again" I say.

I cannot remember if I catch the second attempt or if I miss. It doesn't matter. All I remember is the pure exhilaration of being at top speed, every part of me attuned to the flight of the disc, and my ability to predict, track, and execute the grab. I am laughing, I am joyful and I cannot wipe the smile off of my face if I tried. He is also smiling. I have forgotten everything else in life in that moment. Play. *Flow.* A whole book and career of dedicated research by Mihaly Csikszentmihalyi goes into this concept that brings joy and happiness to people's lives. The Saint's job was to help people find flow, and to find themselves in the process. Again, if that doesn't make a saint, I do not know what does.

He used to play a lot more, but in the last few years, his life had limited his ability to play to the extent he desired. What amazed me though, was he never let his limitations become someone else's. What I mean is, just because he couldn't do something didn't mean he would stop encouraging others. It was beautiful and painful to witness. I knew how much he loved to play, and I longed for the day we could all play together.

One day I show up to work early and it had snowed about four inches. I find him lacing up sleds to be pulled. "What are we doing?" I ask.

"I thought we could go sledding today. It's the perfect amount for the kids to run around and pull each other." he replies. This almost feels like a joke to me. Am I seriously going

WONDER AND THE SAINT

to play with sleds for a whole day and get paid to do this? He grabs a shovel.

"What's that for?" I ask.

"Building jumps." he replies without a thought.

"Building jumps?" I think. Who gets to build jumps in the snow during work? Ever?

That day I heard young men shrieking in high pitched shrills of delight as they ran or were pulled by their friends. Young men typically don't shriek, because it would be "uncool." However, when you experience pure joy, you no longer recall what is "cool" or not. You simply are. I saw smiles plastered across the face of almost every child. I couldn't stop smiling myself as I sprinted back and forth across the field with delight. I pulled the Saint in a sled, too. I think that even though he couldn't experience the snow in the way he desired, our joy was enough of a reminder that day of why he does what he does.

"Do you want play?" he asks me.

I think, "Not only do I want to play more in my life because of you, I want to laugh and encourage others to play more, too." Thank you Saint. I think I had forgotten how to play. You reminded me that I am meant to play and that my life is more wonderful when I do.

"Do you want to play?" I ask my children. Their smiles and my own are enough of an answer.

1. Do I make time to play?

2. What is a mode of play I enjoy?

3. How can I encourage and incorporate play into my life?

LESSON 9

. . . .

"Build People Up - Strong is Sensitive"

When I came to the Saint, my wondering mind came ever more alive with each question he patiently answered. I had a lot to learn as I was entering his field of expertise, not my own. He took his time. Being a skilled teacher, he taught me everything I needed to know. Coming from a different but similar field of expertise, I could have missed opportunities to learn and grow from the Saint. Even though I knew a lot about human movement, I recognized the Saint knew many things I didn't, and it was in being open to growth and recognizing each other's gifts that we grew.

On occasion I asked the same question multiple times, needed help with a task he had already shown me, or couldn't figure something out at all. There were even a few times where the answer was blatantly obvious. He never diminished me, or made me feel "less than" during those interactions where the answer seemed clear.

For example, one day I was having trouble with the audio headset that connects to the speaker. I thought I had everything turned on and plugged in. He simply said, "Let's start with the power source first, and then go from there." Sure enough, I had plugged it in, but not flipped on the power source. It was a simple and obvious fix. He did not laugh at me, or speak any undermining or sarcastic comments. It was like he knew that if I missed something obvious, there was probably a good reason for it. It wasn't his job to make things more difficult. It was his job to build people up.

There were many times I asked questions of which the Saint didn't know the answer. This was one of my favorite things. He would say, "I don't know, let's go find out!" and we would go find out! We would go, call, or find someone who he thought should know the answer. I had never really met someone whose wonder similarly matched mine, or who responded to my questions with more questions. Every question that was patiently and thoughtfully answered allowed us to go deeper into questioning and understanding. I felt safe, which continued to open up the possibility of greater trust and learning. I could call the Saint right now with a question and he would receive me. If he knows the answer, he will tell me. If he doesn't, we will go find out, together.

One day when we were teaching a lesson, the reflective question was, "What is one thing you love most about yourself?" The Saint stood in front of the class and told everyone that what he loved most about himself was his sensitivity. My heart hurt. I have never witnessed a man stand in front of a group and take pride in his sensitivity. It was a paradigm shift. He was sensitive—incredibly sensitive. Instead of seeing his sensitivity as a negative as can be done in our society where "boys don't cry," he saw it as what was beautiful about himself. He made sensitive strong and beautiful. The healthy environment the Saint created enabled others to flourish—myself included. Our ability to empathize, care, and have deep compassion made so much more available.

As I mentioned earlier, vulnerability was difficult for me, and the word sensitive in itself was a struggle. Our friendship allowed me to enter into sensitivity and vulnerability. It was in sharing these moments together that we grew deeper in understanding. Now I can be sensitive, vulnerable and speak from my heart. Strong is sensitive.

1. Do I feel safe to ask questions?

2. Do I build people up around me?

3. How do I receive questions, am I sensitive to my needs and those of others?

LESSON 10

. . . .

"Turn it Up"

"Turn it up!" he says. "I like this song."

"Turn it up?" I think. I'm not sure if anybody has ever spoken these words aloud to me. I've heard, "Turn it down" and "You're kind of loud" and "That's too loud." "Turn it up?" That was a new one for me. Turn it up? I smile. I turn the music up. Is this for real? Am I really listening to my favorite music, with a friend, at work, with people dancing to the beat, smiling, and moving with joy? Okay Saint, I will turn it up—not just the music, but everything I've been turning down and holding back for so many years—just in case it wasn't what someone else wanted to hear. You wanted to hear, you received me, encouraged me, and celebrated with me. You helped me recognize my gifts, encouraged me to share them, and helped me find and strengthen my voice. "Find a publisher!" you said, as I trusted you with my early written works. You are the reason this exists. You said "Turn it up" and I listened.

I am sitting near a beach this summer and my uncle and a few of his friends are gathered for a weekend guy's retreat. They are listening to some classic rock. It's good music. I love music. I walk over toward the music. "This is great music." I say. "Would you mind sharing it with all of us and turning it up?"

They look at me with *wonder.* "Nobody's ever told us to turn it up before! We thought you were coming over here to say turn it down." I see the sparkle in their eyes, I know the feeling when someone says, "Turn it up."

They turn up the music. I dance and sing as I'm walking away. I want to be a person who encourages others to turn it up. I have seen the shadow cast across the eyes when someone comes to share their joy and it is dismissed. I think we can all relate to a time where we were not received. How many times will we attempt to share before we silence our voice or harden our hearts for good? I want to be someone who receives other's joys, celebrates with them and encourages them to "Turn it up!"

1. What aspect of my life do I need to turn up?

2. How can I encourage others to turn up aspects of their lives?

3. Do I make time to listen?

CONCLUSION-LAUGH

Every day I spent with the Saint, no matter what was going on, he made me laugh. I don't mean a giggle or smile. I mean a full belly laugh. Each time I laughed like this, it made me feel younger. Sharing laughter together was healing and restorative. I never really knew if the Saint was joking or serious. You might think that sounds frustrating and there were moments when it was, but more often than not it just made me more curious. It was even more hilarious once I figured out something was a joke, but it did take extra confirmation when he was serious. Fortunately, we didn't spend too much time being serious.

I am not as good at making the Saint laugh as he is at making me laugh. We got better at it together over the year. He took his job seriously. He put great effort, preparation, and work into all that he did, but he didn't take himself too seriously. It was delightful to be a part of a mission driven, hard-working team full of laughter and joy.

At the beginning of this book I introduced the Saint and Wonder, but as our time together grew, something changed.

We were standing in our office one day and he said, "I was reading a book about saints and I thought of you…" I cannot recall the rest of what he said. My mind fixated on the part about him speaking the word "saint" in the same sentence as me. Whoa.

What if I am the Saint, and he is Wonder? What if we are both? At the beginning of our time together, I thought I was there to help him and he was there to teach me. That's when I finally understood, it was our togetherness, teamwork and friendship that made everything possible. Though we were both leaders in our own way, it was when we came together and inspired each other that our potential was magnified. With teachable spirits, open hearts and minds anything is possible! It doesn't matter if you identify with the Saint or with Wonder— in each of us both exist. Perhaps you are Wonder or the Saint in someone else's story?

1. Who are the Saints in my life?

2. Who are the Wonders?

3. Who will I share the journey with?

Thank you! We are grateful that you joined
us on our journey. Together we rise!

THE BEGINNING